Note to Parents

Reading books together can be one of the most pleasurable activities you share with your child. Young children love to spend time with their parents, and the opportunity to be the focus of your undivided attention. To get the most out of reading together, try to find a relaxed time that suits your family. Remember, reading should be fun, so show your enthusiasm and this will transfer to your child. If he or she is wriggling away, leave it for another occasion.

First Time Stories show familiar situations from everyday life that young children can relate to easily. Repetition helps children understand, so I suggest you read this book together more than once. You can use the story as a chance to talk about similar situations in your own child's life. As you read, follow the words with your finger to show the connection of the written word to what you are saying. Encourage your child's imagination if he or she wants to tell a different story from the pictures. Above all, enjoy reading together!

Eileen Hayes
Parenting Consultant to the NSPCC

It's My Turn!

Heather Maisner

ILLUSTRATED BY Kristina Stephenson

KINGFISHER

One morning, Amy and Ben's friends came over to play. Mum and Dad put up a tent in the garden, then they went indoors to work on the house.

Amy and her friend Lucy filled
the tent with teddy bears.

"Let's have a teddy bears' tea
party," said Amy, and they ran
indoors to get the tea set.

"Honk, honk! Honk, honk," Ben cried. "Here comes the dumper truck." He pulled open the tent flaps and unloaded his cars into the tent.

"Toot, toot! Toot, toot," his friend George sang out, pushing the teddies aside.

"Now let's get the tractors," said Ben, and they raced back to the house.

Amy and Lucy carried the tea tray
carefully along the garden path.
Amy opened the tent flaps and
cried, "Ben, what have you done?"

Ben rushed out of the house with his arms full of tractors.

"Out of the way," he called. "Here come the tractors."

"But the teddies are having a tea party," said Amy.

"They can't. This is my garage."

"It isn't."

"It is."

"Mum!" howled Amy.

Mum came hurrying up the garden path.

"Calm down," she said. "Let's see how we can sort this out so you can all play in the tent."

"The teddies were here first," Amy said quickly.

"Then suppose the teddies have their tea party now," said Mum. "And the cars go in there later."

Everyone agreed and they all helped carry the cars out of the tent.

The children asked if they could have lunch in the tent. As soon as Dad put down the pizza, Amy began piling it onto her plate.

"Amy's taking too much," Ben complained.

"I'm hungry," said Amy.

"So am I. I want more." Ben reached for the food on Amy's plate.

"There's plenty for everyone," said Dad, sharing the pizza equally between them. Then they all counted together as he placed ten strawberries in each bowl.

After lunch, Amy and Ben played on the computer while George and Lucy stood watching.

George said, "I want a go," and tried to take Ben's controls.

"Get off," Ben cried, pushing him aside.

"But we want to play too," Lucy moaned, reaching in front of Amy

"Go away," Amy shrieked. "We haven't finished."

Mum rushed in and asked, "If everyone wants to have a go, what do you suppose you could do?" They all frowned. "We could take it in turns," Amy suggested.

"Good," said Mum. "And you could time how long each person plays, so you all have fun."

Later, the boys raced upstairs. As they passed Amy's bedroom, George pointed to a pretty wooden box on the bed and asked, "What's that?"

"Amy's jewellery box," said Ben. "Do you want to see?"
Soon Ben, George and Figaro were dressed in jewellery
from head to toe.

They scampered outside and pranced around the tent.
"That's mine! Give it back," Amy shouted. "Dad!
Come quickly!"

Dad hurried up the path and asked the boys, "How do you think you'd feel if someone took your favourite cars?"

"Very, very angry," said Ben.

"Me too," said George.

"Well, that's how Amy feels right now," Dad said. "So what do you think you should do?"

"Give it back, I suppose," Ben mumbled, as they both took off the jewellery.

"Isn't there a game you could all play together?" Dad asked.

"We could play snakes and ladders," suggested Lucy.

"Or catch!" said Amy.

"No, snap," said George.

"What about hide-and-seek?" said Ben.
But nobody moved.

"I know," said Lucy, "let's have a treasure hunt."

"Yes!" cried Amy. "My jewellery can be the treasure."

"And my cars can be ships and we can be pirates," said Ben.

"And Figaro's our tiger. Yippee! Let's go!" shouted George.

Soon the garden echoed with shrieks and cries as they hunted for treasure and the tent became a castle, then a cabin, then an underground cave.

When Mum and Dad finished
working on the house, they went
out to the garden.

"It's very quiet out here,"
said Mum. They walked
up to the tent and
pulled back the flap.

Lucy, Amy, George
and Ben were curled up
together, falling asleep.

Amy opened one eye and
said, "Thanks for the tent.
We had a fantastic day."

The publisher thanks Eileen Hayes, Parenting Advisor to the NSPCC,
for her kind assistance in the development of this book.

For Nattie and Ollie – H.M.
For Guy, Joshua and Alexandra – K.S.

KINGFISHER
An imprint of Kingfisher Publications Plc
New Penderel House, 283-288 High Holborn
London WC1V 7HZ
www.kingfisherpub.com

First published by Kingfisher 2004
2 4 6 8 10 9 7 5 3 1

Text copyright © Heather Maisner 2004
Illustrations copyright © Kristina Stephenson 2004

A CIP catalogue record for this book
is available from the British Library.

ISBN 0 7534 0998 4

Printed in Singapore
1TR/0704/TWP/PICA(PICA)/150MA